JUL 2008

EDGE
BOOKS™

DRAWING COOL STUFF

HOW TO DRAW

UNREAL
SPACESHIPS

by Aaron Sautter

illustrated by Brian Bascle

Capstone
press®

Mankato, Minnesota

WELCOME!

You probably picked this book because you love out-of-this-world spaceships. Or you picked it because you like to draw. Whatever the reason, get ready to dive into the world of unreal spaceships!

People have dreamed about traveling to the stars for hundreds of years. Long before the first rockets were ever launched, people imagined what kinds of spaceships we might travel in someday. From simple rocket ships and flying saucers to gigantic battleships, spaceships can be any shape or size imaginable.

This book is just a starting point. Once you've learned how to draw the different spaceships in this book, you can start drawing your own. Let your imagination run wild, and see what kinds of crazy alien spaceships you can create!

To get started, you'll need some supplies:

1. First you'll need drawing paper. Any type of blank, unlined paper will do.

2. Pencils are the easiest to use for your drawing projects. Make sure you have plenty of them.

3. You have to keep your pencils sharp to make clean lines. Keep a pencil sharpener close by. You'll use it a lot.

4. As you practice drawing, you'll need a good eraser. Pencil erasers wear out very fast. Get a rubber or kneaded eraser. You'll be glad you did.

5. When your drawing is finished, you can trace over it with a black ink pen or thin felt-tip marker. The dark lines will really make your work stand out.

6. If you decide to color your drawings, colored pencils and markers usually work best. You can also use colored pencils to shade your drawings and make them more lifelike.

MARTIAN MISSILE

Who said there's no life on Mars? In the future, people may be living there. The Martian Missile will be the fastest and cheapest way to travel to the red planet. It's not very comfy, but the hibernation pods will make the trip seem really short!

After drawing this ship, try it again as it lands on Mars!

STEP 1

STEP 2

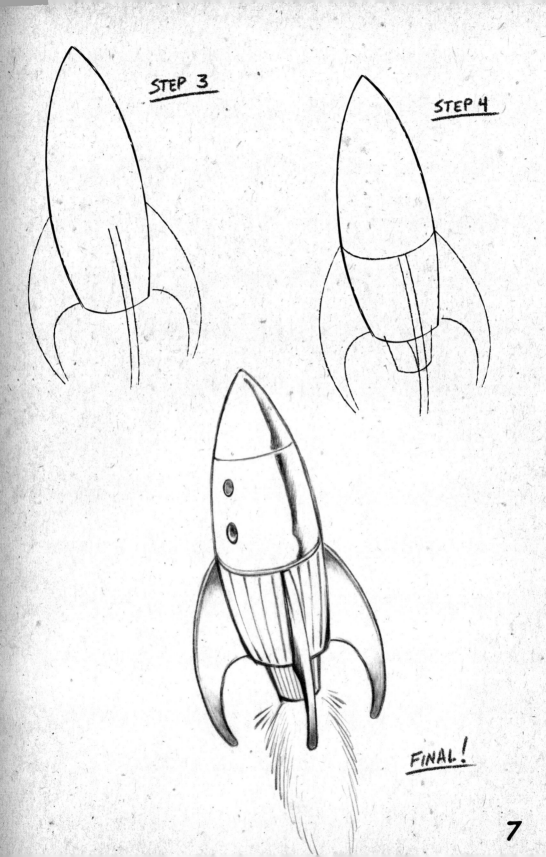

STEP 3

STEP 4

FINAL!

7

SLYTH SAUCER

Have you ever seen a UFO? If so, maybe you saw a Slyth Saucer checking out planet Earth. These ships might seem scary, but there's really nothing to worry about. Most Slyth are only here to look for a good vacation spot!

After practicing this ship, try showing it flying over your town!

STEP 1

STEP 2

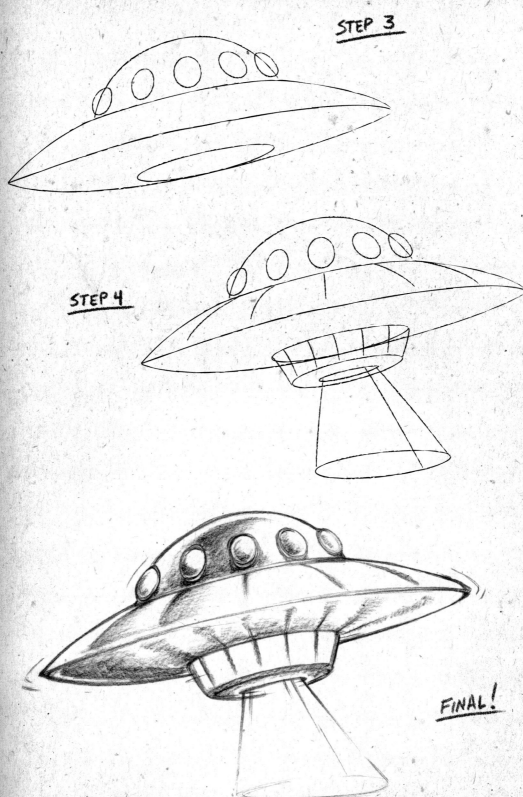

STEP 3

STEP 4

FINAL!

9

FONTANA RACER

Someday, crowded highways won't be a problem. Drivers of the future will take to the air in vehicles like the Fontana Racer. This sporty ship can race up to 800 miles per hour. You can fly from New York to Los Angeles in only a few hours and still be back in time for dinner.

When you're done with this ship, try giving it some cool paint designs!

STEP 1

STEP 2

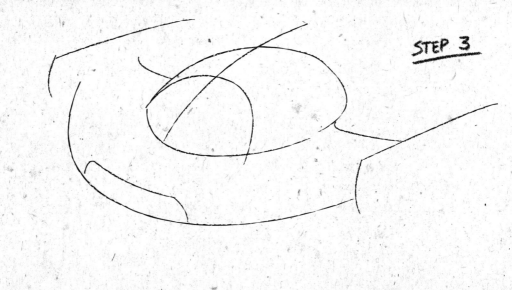

STEP 3

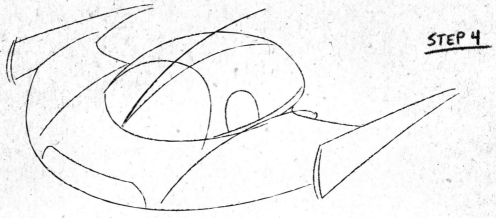

STEP 4

FINAL!

BELKO BOOMERANG

The Belko Boomerang is fast, easy to fly, and useful for almost any need. It can be used to carry passengers between star systems. Or it can be used as a freighter to haul valuable cargo. The Belkonians have even used them as fighters in their battle fleet.

After drawing this ship, try it again as it flies over an alien planet!

STEP 1

STEP 2

12

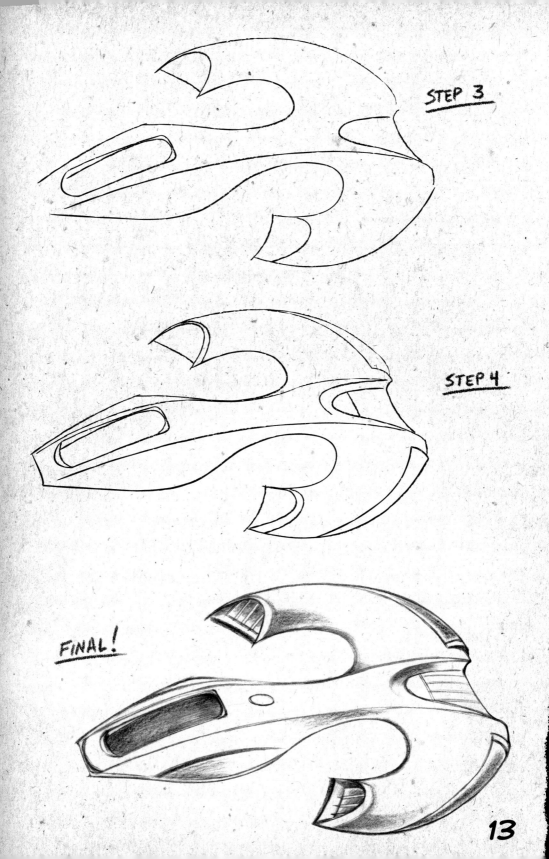

STEP 3

STEP 4

FINAL!

13

H-WING RAPTOR

The H-Wing Raptor is specially designed for space tourists visiting the asteroid belt. Its unique shape lets it easily fly between large asteroids and chunks of floating rock. Raptors are also useful for short trips between the moons of Jupiter.

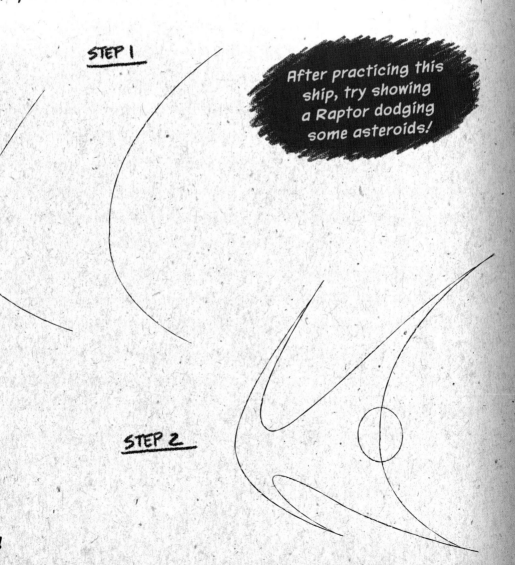

STEP 1

After practicing this ship, try showing a Raptor dodging some asteroids!

STEP 2

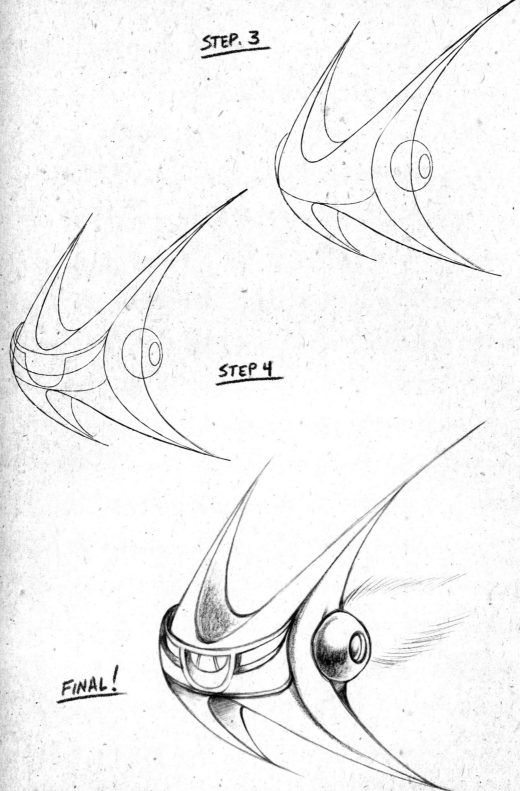

STEP. 3

STEP 4

FINAL!

15

VESPAN STINGER

The Vespan Alliance flies the best starfighters in the galaxy. The Stinger is based on the giant silver hornet found on the planet Vespa. It is fast, maneuverable, and has three powerful laser cannons that rarely miss their target.

After drawing this fighter, be sure to try out the space battle on page 26!

STEP 1

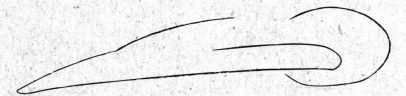

STEP 2

STEP 3

STEP 4

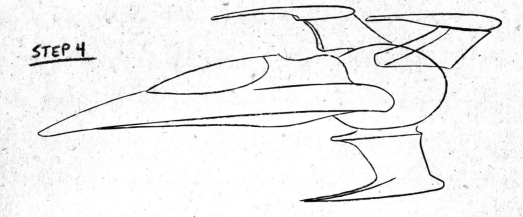

FINAL!

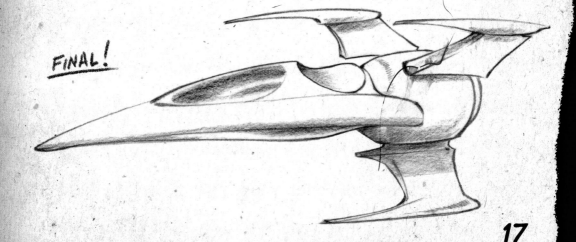

DARKLYTE SABER

The Darklyte Saber is the Falcian Empire's combat fighter. It has three solar panels to power its huge blaster weapon. The Saber is small and fast, but can't take much damage. It attacks in huge numbers to gain an advantage in combat.

When you're done drawing this ship, try it again facing off against another fighter!

STEP 1

STEP 2

18

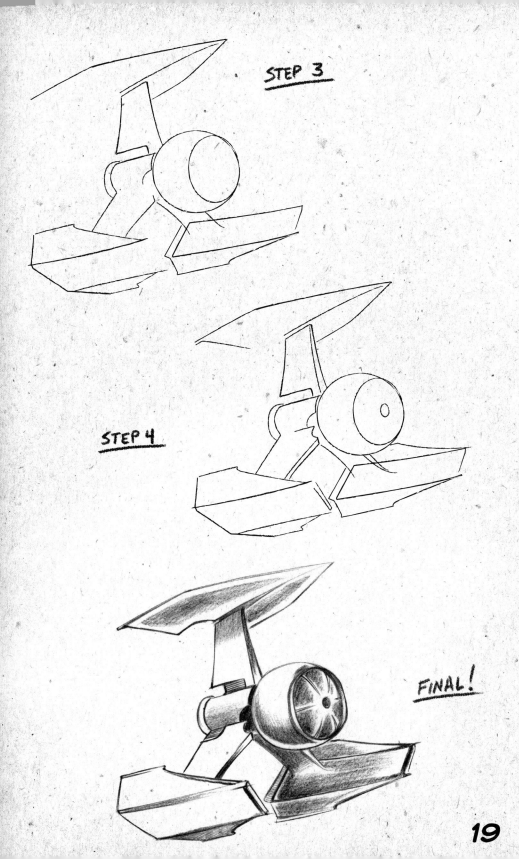

STEP 3

STEP 4

FINAL!

19

STARLITE FREIGHTER

Before the war of 2710, Starlite Freighters were used to transport fragilian ore. But now the ships are mostly used by pirates. Starlite Freighters don't look very impressive, but they are faster and better armed than they appear.

After drawing this ship, try creating your own space freighter design!

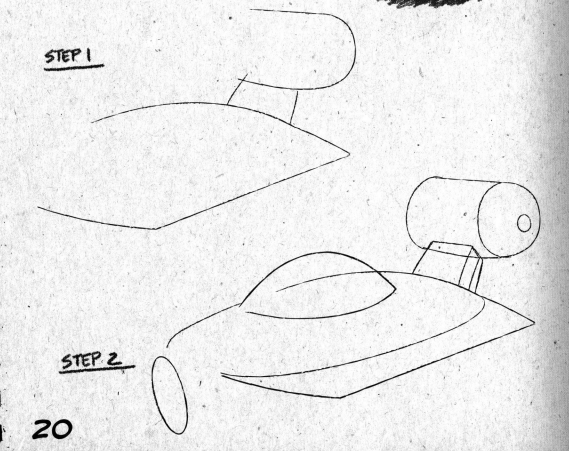

STEP 1

STEP 2

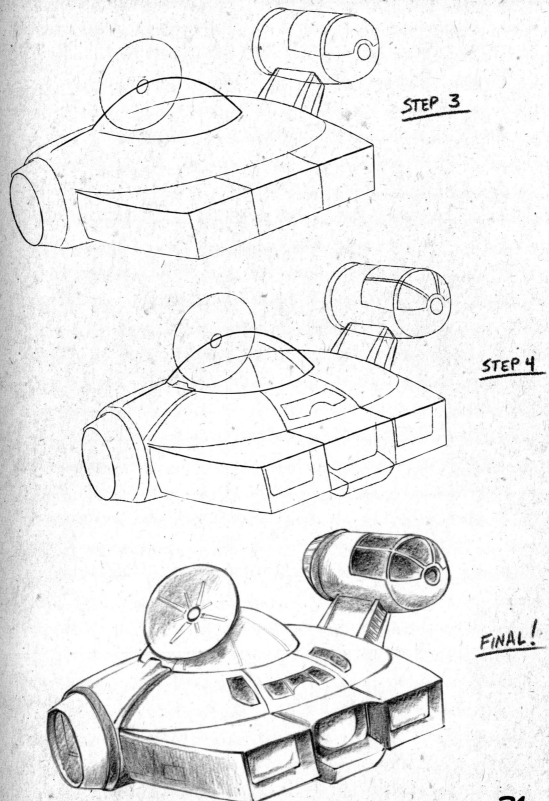

STEP 3

STEP 4

FINAL!

21

SS-8 PLANET JUMPER

Today's small probes take months just to reach the closest planets. But future explorers can use the SS-8 Planet Jumper to travel across the solar system in only a few days. Scientists will be able to learn more about the planets than ever before.

After drawing this ship, try it again as it explores the rings of Saturn!

STEP 1

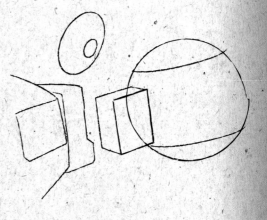

STEP 2

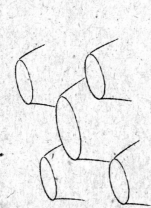

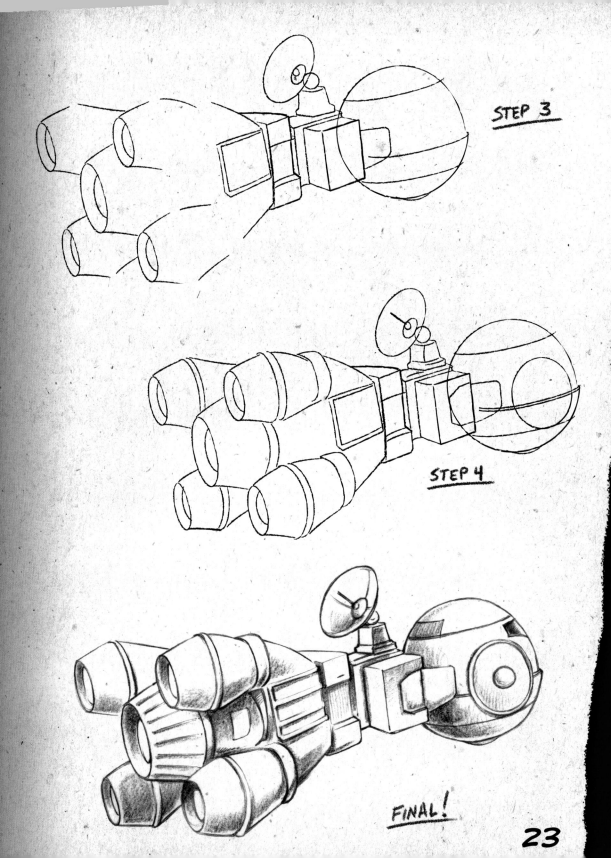

STEP 3

STEP 4

FINAL!

23

ARES BATTLE CRUISER

When the hordes of Gorgo-2 began invading neighboring planets, it was up to the people of Truska to fight back. The Truskans built the Ares Battle Cruiser strong enough to withstand the swarming Gorgites. Once the huge battleship reached Gorgo-2, the war ended quickly.

When you're done drawing this ship, try showing it in battle over Gorgo-2!

STEP 1

STEP 2

STEP 3

STEP 4

FINAL!

25

BATTLE STATIONS!

The Falcian Empire began taking over planets and moons during the Minos Mining Conflict of 2365. Since then, the Empire has spread like a disease through the galaxy. Now the only hope for freedom lies with the Vespan Alliance. Their Stingers are the only fighters that can outrun and outshoot the Empire's Darklyte Sabers.

After you've mastered this space battle, try it again with some of the other ships from this book!

STEP 1

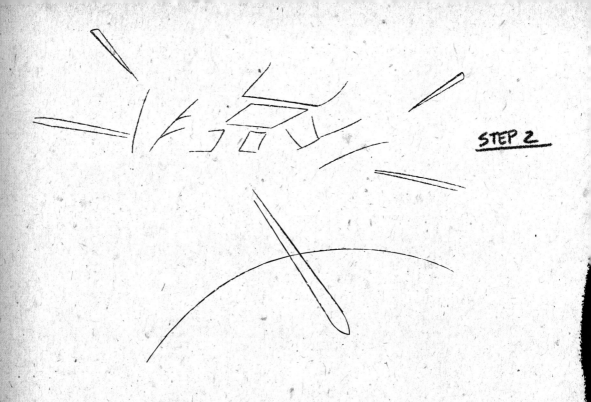

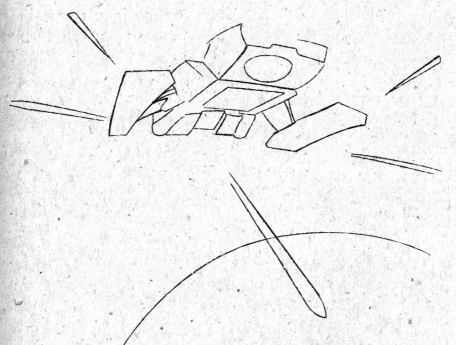

TO FINISH THIS DRAWING,
TURN TO THE NEXT PAGE!

STEP 6

FINAL!

29

GLOSSARY

alliance (uh-LY-uhnss) — an agreement between groups to work together

asteroid (AS-tuh-roid) — a large space rock that moves around the Sun

freighter (FRAY-tuhr) — a ship that carries goods

hibernation (hye-bur-NAY-shuhn) — a period of time spent in a deep sleep

maneuverable (muh-NOO-ver-uh-buhl) — able to move easily

probe (PROHB) — a small vehicle used to explore objects in outer space

solar panel (SOH-lur PAN-uhl) — a flat surface that collects sunlight and turns it into power

UFO (YOO EF OH) — an object in the sky thought to be a spaceship from another planet; UFO is short for Unidentified Flying Object.

unique (yoo-NEEK) — one of a kind

READ MORE

Sautter, Aaron. *How to Draw Disgusting Aliens.* Drawing Cool Stuff. Mankato, Minn.: Capstone Press, 2008.

Visca, Curt. *How to Draw Cartoon Spacecraft and Astronauts in Action.* A Kid's Guide to Drawing. New York: PowerKids Press, 2004.

Walsh, Patricia. *Space Vehicles.* Draw It! Chicago: Heinemann, 2006.

INTERNET SITES

FactHound offers a safe, fun way to find Internet sites related to this book. All of the sites on FactHound have been researched by our staff.

Here's how:
1. Visit *www.facthound.com*
2. Choose your grade level.
3. Type in this book ID **1429613025** for age-appropriate sites. You may also browse subjects by clicking on letters, or by clicking on pictures and words.
4. Click on the **Fetch It** button.

FactHound will fetch the best sites for you!

INDEX